MY EX-FRIEND SETH
Dialogs From a Friendship

Paul Tonnes

MY EX-FRIEND SETH
Dialogs From a Friendship

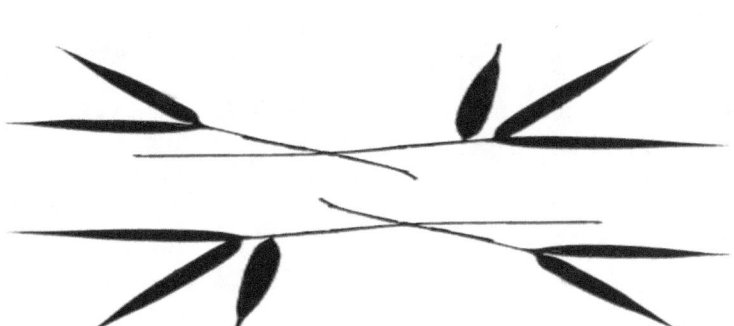

My Ex-Friend Seth
Dialogs From a Friendship

Ex-friend Books
ISBN-13: 978-0692547496
ISBN-10: 0692547495

www.paultonnes.com
Email: paultonnes@nwfirst.com

Printing/manufacturing information for this book may be
found on the last page.

Acknowledgements

Of course, there is Seth Novak, who in-spired this whole mess. Thank you, Seth, you're the best ex-friend I've ever had. Huge thanks go to Marsha Redwood, my editor and truest non-ex-friend. Thanks also to my partner David Poston, whose I-don't-get-it comments are sometimes helpful but mostly wrong.

MY EX-FRIEND SETH
Dialogs From a Friendship

ME
Wanna stop in and get some coffee?

MY EX-FRIEND SETH
I can't go to that Starbucks anymore. The baristas always give me the fish eye.

ME
Why? Are your orders too complex?

MY EX-FRIEND SETH
Not really. I just order free ice water and ask for the restroom code.

MY EX-FRIEND SETH
I just upgraded to Windows 10.

ME
How did it go?

MY EX-FRIEND SETH
Didn't meet my expectations.

ME
How come?

MY EX-FRIEND SETH
Well, I still have a pile of dirty laundry and no girlfriend.

MY EX-FRIEND SETH
You are doing your push-ups all wrong.

ME
Oh really.

MY EX-FRIEND SETH
You should exhale while pushing back up, so the air propels your head right off the floor, like a rocket. It works for me.

ME
That only works for people full of hot air.

MY EX-FRIEND SETH
Who are your favorite artists?

ME
Oh, probably Leonardo, Raphael, Donatello, and Michelangelo.

MY EX-FRIEND SETH
Haha. Those are the Teenage Mutant Ninja Turtles. Who are your favorites really?

ME
Titian.

MY EX-FRIEND SETH
Gesundheit.

ME

What are you doing for International Yoga Day?

MY EX-FRIEND SETH

I'm going to the Yoga Smackdown.

ME

It's a competition?

MY EX-FRIEND SETH

Yeah, well, I don't know. But they'd better get ready for my Ass-kicking Archer, my Down Dog Destroyer, my Mean Meditation, my Crazy Crow, and my Cold Corpse!

MY EX-FRIEND SETH
Who is your ex-friend Seth, anyway?

ME
Just my ex-friend, Seth.

MY EX-FRIEND SETH
I mean he's kinda funny, kinda smart, but mostly clueless.

ME
Yep.

ME
Says here that sit-ups don't burn belly fat.

MY EX-FRIEND SETH
Yeah, but you should do them anyway.

ME
Why?

MY EX-FRIEND SETH
So you get muscles to hold all your fat in.

MY EX-FRIEND SETH
Well, I've just about had it with science!

ME
Why?

MY EX-FRIEND SETH
First they downgrade Pluto from a planet
to an ordinary space rock, even though it is
the awesomest planet EVER. So they send
an expensive space ship to it to prove that
it's a lame space rock. Then they "discover"
that it's really awesome after all, with
craters and ice mountains and stuff, but
REFUSE to make it a planet again.

ME
Exasperating.

MY EX-FRIEND SETH
Who's the guy in charge of science anyway?
We should throw 'em out of office.

MY EX-FRIEND SETH
How did your doctor appointment go?

ME
I have a new doctor, just out of med school. He's really young. I gave him a lollipop at the end of my appointment as a reward for being good.

MY EX-FRIEND SETH
I spent the afternoon twirling a sign by the side of the road for extra money.

ME
How much did you make?

MY EX-FRIEND SETH
Nothing.

ME
What did the sign say?

MY EX-FRIEND SETH
Nothing.

ME
If it doesn't say anything, it's not a sign.

MY EX-FRIEND SETH
I took it as a sign.

MY EX-FRIEND SETH
I want a cactus.

ME
Why?

MY EX-FRIEND SETH
Because taking care of a cactus would be good practice for having a girlfriend.

MY EX-FRIEND SETH
I'm having an ethical dilemma.

ME
About?

MY EX-FRIEND SETH
Social protocol says that I should wish you "happy birthday," because it's your birthday. But I'm your ex-friend, so it seems I'm under no obligation to wish you anything.

ME
Use this new ethics app. It's called iCantEven.

MY EX-FRIEND SETH
Give me your phone. *(typing)* It says I don't need to.

ME
Problem solved.

MY EX-FRIEND SETH
I bet you wish you had a twin as AWESOME
as my brother, Sean!

ME
Yep. And so does Sean.

MY EX-FRIEND SETH
I'm doing a new spiritual renewal thing.

ME
Fasting?

MY EX-FRIEND SETH
Sort of. For an entire week, I'm going to abstain from the internet.

ME
You should live-tweet your experience.

MY EX-FRIEND SETH
Good idea! And I'll Instagram pics of me not using it.

MY EX-FRIEND SETH
Ha! I won. You are toast! You're creamed spinach!

ME
What was your score?

MY EX-FRIEND SETH
Um, 128.

ME
I got 92.

MY EX-FRIEND SETH
YES! You are burnt toast!

ME
But in putt putt golf, the lowest score wins. So you're creamed spinach on burnt toast!

MY EX-FRIEND SETH
I'm hungry all of the sudden.

MY EX-FRIEND SETH
I got 100% on my robotics test today.

ME
You're not that smart. Did you cheat?

MY EX-FRIEND SETH
Well, sort of. I built a robot and told it to take my test.

ME

GMOs are everywhere. You just can't avoid them no matter how hard you try.

MY EX-FRIEND SETH

Seems at your age you'd be happy with any orgasms, genetically modified or otherwise.

ME
Are you going to watch the Super Bowl?

MY EX-FRIEND SETH
I dunno. Who's on it?

ME
You're not "on" the Super Bowl, you're "in" it.

MY EX-FRIEND SETH
I'm in it?!

ME
Don't be difficult.

MY EX-FRIEND SETH

I'm knitting a sweater.

ME

Where did you get the yarn?

MY EX-FRIEND SETH

Not using yarn. I'm using duct tape and lint.

ME

That's not knitting.

MY EX-FRIEND SETH

Then what is it?

ME

Dumb.

MY EX-FRIEND SETH
If I was a vegetarian, I'd still eat bacon.

ME
Then you wouldn't be a vegetarian.

MY EX-FRIEND SETH
You have a problem with that?

MY EX-FRIEND SETH
Let's practice our annoying Facebook statuses. I'll go first. "I always wondered what the ER near my house looked like from the inside."

ME
"Today I'm going to work, then I'm working, then coming home and making dinner, then going to bed."

MY EX-FRIEND SETH
"I'm cleaning out my friend list today so if you don't get my posts tomorrow..."

ME
"Totally spending August/September in Spain, while our penthouse is remodeled."

MY EX-FRIEND SETH
"My ex-friend Seth blah blah blah."

ME
That's just mean.

ME

How did you sleep last night?

MY EX-FRIEND SETH

I dreamed that you dreamed that I dreamed
a dream.

ME

What was I dreaming in the dream of me
dreaming of you?

MY EX-FRIEND SETH

You asked me how I slept.

ME

I paid $50 to get my BMI measured in a dunk tank.

MY EX-FRIEND SETH

What was the result?

ME

I'm fat.

MY EX-FRIEND SETH

Well, I coulda told you that for 25 bucks.

ME

My eye doctor says I have presbyopia.

MY EX-FRIEND SETH

You can't have that 'cause you're Episcopa-
lian.

ME

That's what I said!

MY EX-FRIEND SETH

You tell 'em, old man.

ME

Let's sing a Christmas carol. I'll start and you join in. *(sings)* "Silent night, holy night."

MY EX-FRIEND SETH
(sings)
All was calm, till this song
Onion version, Julia Child
Holy moley, Tinder is wild
Streets are made of green peas
Streets are made of green peas.

ME

You don't know this one, do you?

MY EX-FRIEND SETH

That's how I learned it.

ME

I love you.

MY EX-FRIEND SETH

I love you, too.*

ME

Asterisk? Oh no, here it comes.

MY EX-FRIEND SETH

*Terms and conditions. The party of the first part (I) makes no warranty expressed or implied regarding the party of the second part (you) in any matter other than the condition stated in the declarative (love). Riders may be attached to the declarative (mountain high, river deep) at the discretion of the party of the first part. However, said rider is included for aesthetic and poetic reasons only and should not be construed as a substantive or actionable. No reverse declarative is required; silence will be taken as tacit approval. The party of the first part is not responsible for any actions that the party of the second part may take in response to the declarative (hugs, kisses, reverse declarative). The declarative is non-binding and non-transferable. Conditions subject to change without notice.

MY EX-FRIEND SETH
What did you guys do before the internet?

ME
We laughed, we loved, we danced in the rain.

MY EX-FRIEND SETH
No, seriously. How did you email each other?

ME
We printed them out and sent them to the post office.

MY EX-FRIEND SETH
Ah, makes sense. And how did you text?

ME
Texting was talking back then.

ME

It's St. Patrick's Day, and you're not wearing green?

MY EX-FRIEND SETH

I am! Look at my foot.

ME

Yuck, what is that?

MY EX-FRIEND SETH

Gangrene.

ME

That doesn't count.

ME
Do you ever think about your own death?

MY EX-FRIEND SETH
Nope. Never.

ME
Why not?

MY EX-FRIEND SETH
Because I've noticed that death only hap-
pens to other people, not me.

MY EX-FRIEND SETH
With my new smart phone I can: txt a voice,
voice a txt, Facebook a Facetime, Facetime
a face, face some time, email a txt, txt a pic,
pick a txt, share a like, like a share, emote a
con, app an ape, ape a selfie, self a shamey,
pic a txty, and vox a fox.

ME
All I wanna do is make a phone call.

MY EX-FRIEND SETH
What's a phone call?

MY EX-FRIEND SETH
Is that a new haircut?

ME
Uh huh.

MY EX-FRIEND SETH
Amazing!

ME
Thanks.

MY EX-FRIEND SETH
Amazing that no matter what haircut you have, you still look like Phyllis Diller.

MY EX-FRIEND SETH
Do you have any scientist friends?

ME
Yep, lots.

MY EX-FRIEND SETH
Good, 'cause I have lots of Drosophila me-
lanogaster in my kitchen and it would be a
shame to see them go to waste.

MY EX-FRIEND SETH
Times New Roman—from now on I'm going to announce what font I'm using when I talk.

ME
Why?

MY EX-FRIEND SETH
Lucida Handwriting—because I'll be better understood, and besides, it's Rosewood STD Regular—awesome!

ME
Comic Sans—that's stupid.

MY EX-FRIEND SETH
Your lies and deception have got to stop!

ME
What are you talking about?

MY EX-FRIEND SETH
I saw you enter 135 pounds and 32 years old into the machine at the gym.

ME
Relax, everyone lies to those machines. Don't they?

MY EX-FRIEND SETH
I don't ever want to turn 27.

ME
Um, why?

MY EX-FRIEND SETH
A bunch of amazing people died when they were 27—Joplin, Morrison, Cobain.

ME
Don't worry. You're not that amazing.

MY EX-FRIEND SETH
I heard they finally discovered what causes ALS with all the money that Ice Bucket Challenge has raised.

ME
Great news! What is it?

MY EX-FRIEND SETH
Ice water.

MY EX-FRIEND SETH
I'm finishing this quarter of school on a high note.

ME
You got good grades?

MY EX-FRIEND SETH
No, I feel like a castrato.

ME

What are you doing?

MY EX-FRIEND SETH

I'm writing a computer algorithm. It requires three inputs: barometric pressure (in mmHg), temperature (in Celsius), and elevation (in meters).

ME

And the output?

MY EX-FRIEND SETH

How frizzy your hair will be today.

ME
Where are you going?

MY EX-FRIEND SETH
To fly my new drone in the park.

ME
That is so stupid. It's totally illegal and
dangerous. The FAA and the cops are going
to arrest you.

MY EX-FRIEND SETH
Relax, it's the kind with a string.

ME

How are your feet?

MY EX-FRIEND SETH

Oh, you mean my calluses? I went to the dermatologist.

ME

And...

MY EX-FRIEND SETH

She said I have Super Callus Fragilistic Expialidocious.

ME

That sounds atrocious.

MY EX-FRIEND SETH
I can't wait for next summer!

ME
Why? What are you doing?

MY EX-FRIEND SETH
Looking back at this summer with nostal-gia.

MY EX-FRIEND SETH
I heard you can get crabs from the clothes
at the Salvation Army.

ME
It's true.

MY EX-FRIEND SETH
And used crabs are the WORST.

MY EX-FRIEND SETH
I need a Nucleotide Alignment Process.

ME
Huh?

MY EX-FRIEND SETH
A N.A.P. I sleep best while my head is pointing magnetic north and my feet are pointing south.

ME
That is the stupidest thing I ever heard.

MY EX-FRIEND SETH
Help me move the couch.

MY EX-FRIEND SETH
I see you're one of those people.

ME
What people?

MY EX-FRIEND SETH
People who re-load the dishwasher to their own persnickety standards.

ME
I hate myself for that.

MY EX-FRIEND SETH
Watcha reading?

ME
The marginalia that some anonymous student wrote in their copy of Boyd's book about Nabakov's *Pale Fire*, which is Kinbote's commentary on Shade's poem, also named *Pale Fire* (the title of which is taken from a line in Shakespeare's *Timon of Athens*), specifically canto I, which compares pheasant tracks in the snow to dots and arrows pointing backwards, which Boyd helpfully illustrates as .<-- .<-- .

MY EX-FRIEND SETH
Give me the phone.

ME
Why?

MY EX-FRIEND SETH
I'm calling your doctor; it's time to up your meds.

ME
The History Channel is doing shows on swamp people and Bigfoot.

MY EX-FRIEND SETH
That's because they ran out of real history and are waiting for more to happen.

MY EX-FRIEND SETH
I'm making cross stitch wall art, real old fashioned-ish.

ME
What does it say?

MY EX-FRIEND SETH
"Home is where the Wi-Fi is."

MY EX-FRIEND SETH
Some guy on the bus was telling me that submarines are built above the water, you know, on the ground!

ME
And you didn't believe him?

MY EX-FRIEND SETH
Haha, no. Jeez.

ME
Moron.

MY EX-FRIEND SETH
I know, right?

MY EX-FRIEND SETH

"I accept no liability for the content of this dialog, nor for the consequences of any actions taken on the basis of the information provided, unless that information is subsequently confirmed in writing. If you are not the intended recipient, you are notified that disclosing, copying, distributing or taking any action in reliance on the contents of this dialog is strictly prohibited," is how I'm starting all my sentences now, because you can't be too careful these days.

ME

Really? And how do your roommates feel about this?

MY EX-FRIEND SETH

"I accept no liability for the content of this dialog, nor for the consequences of any actions taken on the basis of the information provided, unless that information is subsequently confirmed in writing. If you are not the intended recipient, you are notified that disclosing, copying, distributing or taking any action in reliance on the contents of this dialog is strictly prohibited." Well, there's a lot of eye rolling going on at home.

MY EX-FRIEND SETH
Jesus said you should love your enemies.

ME
Yeah, maybe we should try it.

MY EX-FRIEND SETH
But he didn't say anything about ex-friends, so we're off the hook.

ME
Praise the Lord!

MY EX-FRIEND SETH
I'm going to start using asides in my life.

ME
Good idea. (*aside*: The fool doesn't know that asides only work in the theater, not real life.)

MY EX-FRIEND SETH
I heard that. Besides, "all the world's a stage," so it should work.

ME

I'm getting a whole new wardrobe. Something edgier.

MY EX-FRIEND SETH

You're too round to be edgy.

ME
Who is your favorite actress?

MY EX-FRIEND SETH
That lady on Modern Family.

ME
Oh yeah, Sofia something-or-other.

MY EX-FRIEND SETH
Viagra.

ME
I don't think it's Viagra.

MY EX-FRIEND SETH
She is for me!

MY EX-FRIEND SETH
Don't you think people use the "so-called" "air quotes" too much?

ME
I do. It's a real, "how should I say," "concern" of mine.

MY EX-FRIEND SETH
It's like they have a, "how should I put it," a "quote quota" to fulfill.

ME
I have to wash my face.

(25 minutes later)

MY EX-FRIEND SETH
That took sooooo loooong. What happened?

ME
Exfoliate (physical and chemical), dry, tone,
air dry, serum application, moisturizer,
eye bag eliminator, more moisturizer, and
sun screen.

MY EX-FRIEND SETH
All that and you STILL look 62.

ME
I'm 50.

ME

What makes you think it's OK to take up two parking spaces?

MY EX-FRIEND SETH

Probably my sense of entitlement.

MY EX-FRIEND SETH
I know it's time to wash my gym socks
when—

ME
Please, please don't tell me.

MY EX-FRIEND SETH
—the mold on them kills the fungus on my
feet.

ME

What was your favorite food at Thanksgiving?

MY EX-FRIEND SETH

The Horse Ovaries.

ME

Huh?

MY EX-FRIEND SETH

I mean the Horse d'divorce. No I mean the Hors d'voracious. Hors d'oeuvres! Finally!

ME

You're the only person I know who has to autocorrect his own speech.

ME

How is your new girlfriend; she's from
Russia right?

MY EX-FRIEND SETH

Yeah, and she's super hot. But she sleeps all
the time.

ME

What was her name again?

MY EX-FRIEND SETH

Anesthesia.

ME
I can't find my memory foam pillow.

MY EX-FRIEND SETH
Well, obviously it doesn't work.

ME

How was your day?

MY EX-FRIEND SETH

Great. Nothing happened!

ME

Why is that great?

MY EX-FRIEND SETH

'Cause if something happened, I would have to pin it, post it, wiki it, tumblr it, tweet it, blog it, + it, send it, link it, txt it, skype it, flick it, insta it, tag it, and myspace it. It's exhausting.

ME
What are you doing with Sean for Happy
Siblings Day?

MY EX-FRIEND SETH
I'm making him happy by avoiding him.

MY EX-FRIEND SETH
Gay marriage is going to lead to heartache and protracted embitterment.

ME
Oh really. Why?

MY EX-FRIEND SETH
Because y'all forgot to ask for gay divorce.

ME

Try my homemade sugar cookies. So good,
you'll be overwhelmed!

MY EX-FRIEND SETH
(bites, chews)

Nope. Just whelmed.

MY EX-FRIEND SETH
I've joined a new social network.

ME
really

MY EX-FRIEND SETH
It's for people with short attention spans.
Called Twit. A six character limit and no
capitals or punctuation allowed.

ME
stupid

MY EX-FRIEND SETH
Exactly!

MY EX-FRIEND SETH
Listen to this. Who knew classical music
could ROCK?!

ME
It's great, but it's not classical music.

MY EX-FRIEND SETH
Yeah it is, 'cause they have a violin.

ME
You txt me too much. Cut it out.

MY EX-FRIEND SETH
Waddya mean?

ME
Do not txt me from afar
Do not txt me from a car
If you txt me I will not care
Do not txt me anywhere

MY EX-FRIEND SETH
Can I txt you with a fox?

ME
Not even for a million bucks!

MY EX-FRIEND SETH
LOL, LRA (Lame Rhyme Alert).

MY EX-FRIEND SETH
From now on, you either have to "Like" or
"Comment" on anything I say, à la Facebook.

ME
I like that.

MY EX-FRIEND SETH
Was that a "Comment" or a "Like"?

ME

Eeeeew Seth! Plant a tree.

MY EX-FRIEND SETH

Huh?

ME

Your farts are greenhouse gasses.

MY EX-FRIEND SETH

Gotta love those offsets!

MY EX-FRIEND SETH
Stop biting your fingernails. You're supposed to be on a liquid diet.

ME
Leave me alone.

MY EX-FRIEND SETH
Next thing you know, you'll be gnawing off your arm.

ME

What are you doing?

MY EX-FRIEND SETH

Straightening spaghetti.

ME

Why?

MY EX-FRIEND SETH

'Cause I made too much and I need to get it back in the box.

ME
So the Supreme Court said I can get married in all 50 states!

MY EX-FRIEND SETH
What you gonna do with 50 husbands?

ME

You need to be decisive. You vacillate too much.

MY EX-FRIEND SETH

Well, sometimes I do, and sometimes I don't.

MY EX-FRIEND SETH
I've sold $25 worth of tickets to your show.

ME
My show? What show?

MY EX-FRIEND SETH
Your colonoscopy.

ME
Seth! That's supposed to be a PRIVATE procedure. Good Lord.

MY EX-FRIEND SETH
It's performance art!

ME

Yuck, what is that gelatinous mess in your
bathroom?

MY EX-FRIEND SETH

A jar full of used, disposable contact lenses.
I collect them from the neighbors.

ME

Why?

MY EX-FRIEND SETH

To give to charity.

ME

Thoughtful.

ME
Whatcha thinkin' about?

MY EX-FRIEND SETH
How to sell this "For Sale" sign.

ME
I thought you sold it already?

MY EX-FRIEND SETH
No, I sold the old "For Sale" sign using this new sign. But now I need to sell this new one, too.

ME
I'm wondering how to throw this old garbage can away.

MY EX-FRIEND SETH
I'm going to the gym to do some ab exercises.

ME
What kind of exercises?

MY EX-FRIEND SETH
You know, the normal ones.

ME
Oh, you're doing ab-normals. Figures.

MY EX-FRIEND SETH
Guess what the greatest genetically engineered food is.

ME
What?

MY EX-FRIEND SETH
Heirloom tomatoes.

ME
I don't even know where to begin.

The Scene: My ex-friend Seth at the kitchen sink, with piles of colanders, funnels, sieves, and strainers.

ME

What are you doing?

MY EX-FRIEND SETH

Testing all your strainers to see if they work.

ME

I'm dumbfounded.

MY EX-FRIEND SETH

You'll thank me when it's straining time.

MY EX-FRIEND SETH
Your last art show sold zero paintings. Zilch.

ME
I know.

MY EX-FRIEND SETH
Amazing. Absolutely nothing.

ME
So nothing amazes you?

MY EX-FRIEND SETH
Apparently.

ME
How did you like the symphony last night?

MY EX-FRIEND SETH
I loved every note of it, just not in that order.

MY EX-FRIEND SETH
You are always in a constant state of puzzle-ment.

ME
Probably so. Have you ever seen me when I'm not around you?

MY EX-FRIEND SETH
Um, no.

ME
Q.E.D.

MY EX-FRIEND SETH
What is the one superpower you would like to have?

ME
Invisibility.

MY EX-FRIEND SETH
As a gay man over 50, you already have that.

MY EX-FRIEND SETH

Can you say *Rindfleischetikettierungsüber-wachungsaufgabenübertragungsgesetz*

ME

No.

MY EX-FRIEND SETH

It's German. And there's no reason for you to say it, 'cause you're a vegetarian and it's about meat.

ME
What are you knitting?

MY EX-FRIEND SETH
I'm not knitting. Knitting is only for women.

ME
Then what are you doing with the yarn and knitting needles?

MY EX-FRIEND SETH
3D printing.

MY EX-FRIEND SETH
Try my homemade vegan almond milk.

ME
Yum, that's so good! What's in it?

MY EX-FRIEND SETH
Cream.

MY EX-FRIEND SETH
I'm going to the bank.

ME
Why?

MY EX-FRIEND SETH
To exchange some Washington money for Vermont money.

ME
Let me know how that goes.

ME

I've got a cold that is making me dizzy.

MY EX-FRIEND SETH

You should go to the drug store.

ME

Yeah, I need some cold medicine.

MY EX-FRIEND SETH

No, hair color. That way you won't be a dizzy blond.

(telephone rings)
ME

Hello?

MY EX-FRIEND SETH
I've lost my phone so don't call me.

ME
How are you calling me now?

MY EX-FRIEND SETH
I'm just using friends' phones now.

ME
(incredulous)

What friends?

MY EX-FRIEND SETH
Anybody with a phone is my friend.

ME
Good Lord, this book is heavy.

MY EX-FRIEND SETH
Yeah, Shakespeare was stupid for putting all his plays in one book.

ME
I need to make a change.

MY EX-FRIEND SETH
Face lift? Psychoanalysis? Liposuction?

ME
I was thinking of a haircut.

MY EX-FRIEND SETH
A chicken brain is smaller than your thumb.

ME
Chickens are dumb.

MY EX-FRIEND SETH
But they are smart enough to be good at
being chickens.

ME

I have a stomach ache.

MY EX-FRIEND SETH

You should get a freckle transplant.

ME

A what?

MY EX-FRIEND SETH

A freckle transplant. It's a new thing. Doctors put freckles from normal people into sick people, and then they feel better.

ME

You mean a fecal transplant.

MY EX-FRIEND SETH

Poop! That's just gross. You should get one of those too.

MY EX-FRIEND SETH
I haven't been to my apartment in four days.

ME
Do you miss home?

MY EX-FRIEND SETH
Nope, 'cause anywhere I charge my phone
is home.

MY EX-FRIEND SETH
Ok I'm done.

ME
Done with what?

MY EX-FRIEND SETH
Everything. I've thought every thought,
done every deed—now I'm done.

ME
Only when you're done being done will you
really be done.

And a few that started it all

"—so I took my *second* skateboard out and made a smooth getaway." —Seth Novak

"The only kind of fun I have is weird-fun." —Seth Novak

"It's not that I'm so young, it's just that you're so old." —Seth Novak (19)

"There's really no reason to eat tofu if you eat meat." —Seth Novak

About the Author

Paul Tonnes is an artist whose art doesn't sell. He divides his time between Seattle and No.13 Hercules Buildings, Lambeth London.

MY EX-FRIEND SETH
Aren't you forgetting something?

ME
What?

MY EX-FRIEND SETH
All those fancy literary books say something about the typeface at the back.

ME
Ok. How's this?

<u>A Note on the Type</u>
This book is set in *Chepman*. It was devel-
oped by my friend, polymath Rob
McKaughan. Rob says, "*Chepman*
provides an excellent reading experience
and has a friendly and approachable per-
sonality."

MY EX-FRIEND SETH
Nobody cares that he can do math.